POPPY'S BABIES

Jill Barklem

HarperCollins *Children's Books*

For Lizzie and Peter

For more information visit the Brambly Hedge website at:
www.bramblyhedge.com

First published in Great Britain by
HarperCollins Publishers Ltd in 1994
New edition published in 1996
This edition published by HarperCollins Children's Books in 2018

1 3 5 7 9 10 8 6 4 2

ISBN: 978-0-00-828281-3

HarperCollins Children's Books is a division of HarperCollins Publishers Ltd.

Text and illustrations copyright © Jill Barklem 1994

Visit our website at: www.harpercollins.co.uk

Printed in China

BRAMBLY HEDGE

For many generations, families of mice have made
their homes in the roots and trunks
of the trees of Brambly Hedge,
a dense and tangled hedgerow
that borders the field on the
other side of the stream.

The Brambly Hedge mice lead
busy lives. During the fine weather,
they collect flowers, fruits, berries and nuts from the
Hedge and surrounding fields, and prepare
delicious jams, pickles and preserves that
are kept safely in the Store Stump for
the winter months ahead.

Although the mice work hard, they make
time for fun too. All through the year, they
mark the seasons with feasts and festivities and, whether
it be a little mouse's birthday, an eagerly awaited wedding
or the first day of spring, the mice
welcome the opportunity
to meet and celebrate.

It was the beginning of summer. Outside, the trees were in leaf and sunshine sparkled on the stream. The millwheel turned in the cool shadows of the riverbank and inside the mill Dusty Dogwood was busy grinding the corn for the mice of Brambly Hedge.

Poppy was upstairs trying to persuade her new babies to go to sleep but every time they closed their eyes, the clatter of the mill shook the floorboards and woke them again.

She opened the door to the stairs and a cloud of flour dust blew into her face.

"Dusty, please finish soon. It's time for the babies' nap."

"I'll do my best," he called back.

The babies were still awake when two visitors peeped round the door.

"Do you know that there are ninety-two stairs up
to your kitchen?" gasped Primrose.

"However do you manage with the babies?"
asked Lady Woodmouse, giving Poppy a kiss.

"It's very difficult," Poppy replied. She looked
as though she was about to cry.

"How sweet they are," said Lady Woodmouse.
"This one looks just like Dusty."

"That's Rose. Here is Buttercup, and the little one is Pipkin."

"I can't wait for their Naming Day," said Primrose. "When is it?"

"Just two days away!" said Lady Woodmouse.

At last the millwheels stopped turning and the babies slept. The visitors tiptoed out and Poppy sat down to rest. She was exhausted.

Dusty bagged up the flour and went over to the Store Stump. He found Mr Apple sitting at his workshop door, putting the finishing touches to a wooden mouse on wheels.

Wilfred, who was meant to be helping, was finding it much more amusing to play in the wood shavings.

"Hello, Dusty," said Mr Apple. "How are those babies of yours?"

"Noisy," laughed Dusty, "but great fun. Poppy is not so happy though. The mill is a very inconvenient place to live. It's noisy, dusty and damp and has far too many stairs."

"Come and live at our house," offered Wilfred.
"My mother loves babies."

"Thank you, Wilfred, but I fancy your mother has
enough on her hands with the four of you."

"I wonder what we can do to help Poppy," said
Mr Apple sympathetically.

Dusty returned later in the day to collect some wood for a repair to the mill.

"Come with me," said Mr Apple. Dusty and Wilfred followed him to a little cottage in a hawthorn tree next to the Store Stump.

"I've never noticed this house before," said Dusty.

"It's been empty for years. I use it to keep my timber dry," said Mr Apple.

While Dusty chose a suitable plank, Wilfred peered at an old cooking range.

"Does this still work?" he asked.

"I expect so," said Mr Apple. "It used to be very cosy when my aunt lived here." Suddenly he raised a paw. "Dusty, Wilfred has given me an idea. Suppose we clean the cottage and paint it. Would it suit you and Poppy?"

Dusty thought for a moment and then he said excitedly, "You know, I think it might!"

"Poppy would love this," Dusty said, looking
at a small sunny room. "It's just the right size for
a nursery."

"Let's get everything ready for Naming Day," said
Mr Apple. "Do you think we can keep it a secret?"
He looked pointedly at Wilfred.

"I won't say anything," said Wilfred. "Promise."

Mr Apple and Wilfred
went off to Crabapple Cottage
to tell Mrs Apple about the plan and Dusty hurried
home to help give the babies their bath.

"Look," cried Poppy.
"Buttercup's learnt to crawl."
Dusty lifted her up and
gave her a hug.

"I do wish we lived somewhere else," said Poppy.
"I have to watch them every minute of the day."

Mrs Apple had alerted all the mice along the hedge and early next morning they began to arrive at Mayblossom Cottage with buckets and brooms. The windows were opened wide and the floors swept, sanded and scrubbed. Mrs Apple wiped down the dresser shelves and cleaned out the cupboards and Mrs Toadflax polished the bath. Dusty lit a pile of twigs in each grate to check that the chimneys weren't blocked.

"Now for the whitewash," said Mr Apple. "Do you want to mix it, Wilfred?"

"As soon as the walls are dry, we can start to fetch the furniture from the mill," said Dusty.

"But how can we do that without Poppy seeing?"

"Ah, Mrs Apple's thought of a plan," said Mr Apple.

The next day Lady Woodmouse and Poppy sat
under the hedge, sewing. Bees buzzed in and out
of the flowers in the early morning sunshine and
the scent of hawthorn blossom filled the air.

"There, that quilt's finished," said Lady Woodmouse, putting the last stitch into a yellow flower.

"I've still got Pipkin's gown to make," sighed Poppy. "However am I going to finish it in time?"

"We've had a good idea," said Lady Woodmouse. "Why don't you all come and stay at the Palace with us tonight. We can work on the gowns together and Primrose can help you to dress the babies for Naming Day tomorrow morning."

"That would help Dusty too," said Poppy. "He seems to be very busy at the moment."

By late that afternoon, the cottage was almost ready.
Wilfred put a last coat of whitewash on the nursery
walls and Dusty measured up for the furniture.

"There, everything fits," he said with satisfaction.
"Let's go back to the mill for tea."

"Goodness, whatever have you two been doing?"
asked Poppy, staring at Wilfred's fur.

"Painting," said Wilfred proudly. "I mean…"

"Something for the babies," said Dusty quickly.

"You are a kind mouse, Wilfred," said Poppy.

Up and down Brambly Hedge, the mice were all
busy. In the Palace kitchen, Mrs Crustybread was
making a special cake and her daughter Cicely made
rose petal butter and creamy junket.

Over at Mayblossom Cottage, Mrs Toadflax
had laid the table and was now hanging curtains,
while up in the nursery, Lady Woodmouse unpacked
the three little quilts.

"We're ready to fetch Poppy now," she said.

"Right," said Dusty. "As soon as you're at the
Palace, we'll start to move in the furniture."

Down at the mill, Poppy was busy packing.

"There seems to be so much to take," she said, folding up three little nightgowns. "Perhaps I should stay here after all."

"No, no," said Lady Woodmouse hastily. "Primrose will be so disappointed if you don't come."

Eventually, they managed to get the nappies, bottles, toys, prams and babies down the stairs (all ninety-two of them!) and were ready to set off to the Palace.

The babies loved the journey. Rose gurgled when she saw the stream, Pipkin threw his rattle in the water and when they reached the field, Buttercup tried to get out of the pram.

At the door of Old Oak Palace, Dusty kissed his family goodnight.

"Don't wait up for me," he said, "I've one or two things to sort out before tomorrow."

The babies were bathed and put into their nightgowns. They were so excited by their new surroundings that they didn't want to settle but at last they all fell asleep in the quiet of the hedgerow evening.

Lady Woodmouse lit the lamp, then she and Poppy sat and stitched the last of the lace on to the babies' gowns.

"How peaceful it is here," said Poppy.

As she spoke, a curious squeaking, bumping noise came through the open window.

"Whatever is that?" Poppy asked, startled.

Lady Woodmouse got up quickly and drew the curtains.

"Just Lord Woodmouse tidying up," she said. "We'd better get to bed. We'll need to be up before first light tomorrow."

Very early next morning, all the mice gathered
beneath the hawthorns for the Naming Ceremony.
As dawn broke, Poppy handed Old Vole the first
baby. Primrose held up a cup of dew, freshly
gathered from the flowers, for Old Vole to sprinkle
on the baby's head.

"The buds on the branches blossom and flower,
The blackbirds sing in the leafy bower,
And over the hill comes the rising sun,
To shine on the fields, and on you, little one."

"We name you Rose," said Old Vole, gently.

Just as Old Vole named the last baby Pipkin, the mice heard the patter of raindrops on the leaves.

"Oh dear, we'll all get wet," cried Poppy.

"No, no. Come this way," said Lady Woodmouse. "Bring the babies."

Poppy and Dusty ran towards the Store Stump and Dusty stood aside to let Poppy take shelter in the open door of a cottage.

Poppy found herself in the kitchen. Bright china that looked rather familiar was arranged on the dresser shelves and garlands of flowers hung from newly washed beams.

"What a dear little house," said Poppy.

"Let's look round," said Dusty.

Leaving Primrose in charge of the babies, Poppy and Dusty climbed the stairs.

"It's so cosy," she said as they reached the landing.
"I wonder who lives here?"

Dusty led her to a small room that was warm and
bright. Fresh curtains hung at the windows and
beneath them stood three little cots, each with its
own embroidered quilt. One was pink, one was
yellow and one was blue.

"But Dusty…" she cried.

"Yes," said Dusty, "with love from all your friends in Brambly Hedge. Welcome home!"

Poppy threw her paws round Dusty.

"This is the nicest surprise I've ever had," she said, then she ran downstairs to thank each mouse in turn.

"It's time to cut the cake!" shouted Wilfred.

Everyone was given a large slice and Basil served a summer punch with flowers floating on top. There were cowslip and violet salads, rose petal sandwiches, primrose pottage and meadowsweet tea.

The babies crawled around underfoot and Poppy was glad of Mr Apple's gates on the stairs. Then they were given some cake and got very sticky. Soon Rose began to cry, followed by Buttercup, and Pipkin rolled under the table.

"Poor babies, you're tired," said Poppy. "I'm going to put you into your cots."

The baby mice snuggled under their new quilts and by the time Poppy bent to kiss them, they were fast asleep. She tiptoed back downstairs to join the guests in the kitchen.

Mr Apple proposed a toast.

"To the babies," he whispered, "and their new home."

"To Rose, Buttercup and Pipkin," added Mrs Apple. "Bless their little whiskers."

THE FAR WOODS

THE

THE
CHESTNUT WOODS

Hornbeam
Crabapple
Cottage

THE F

Blackberry Patch

Brambly
Hedge

Rabbit holes.

N